SECRET PIZZA PARTY

To my friends and heroes in magic, who taught me the value
of a story well told and a secret well kept.   —AR

For beautiful Sophia   —DS

ISBN 978-0-545-80106-5

Text copyright © 2013 by Adam Rubin. Illustrations copyright © 2013 by Daniel Salmieri.
All rights reserved. Published by Scholastic Inc., 557 Broadway, New York, NY 10012,
by arrangement with Dial Books for Young Readers, a division of
Penguin Young Readers Group, a member of Penguin Group (USA) LLC,
A Penguin Random House Company. SCHOLASTIC and associated logos are
trademarks and/or registered trademarks of Scholastic Inc.

12 11 10 9 8 7 6 5   16 17 18 19/0

Printed in the U.S.A.   40

First Scholastic printing, September 2014

Designed by Jennifer Kelly
Text set in Octone
The art was created with watercolor, gouache, and color pencil.

SECRET PIZZA PARTY

BY **Adam Rubin**

ILLUSTRATED BY **Daniel Salmieri**

SCHOLASTIC INC.

SILVERMAN'S BEARD STORE

Uncle Mark's PIZZA

USE MIT

All he wants in life is some pizza.

If only he knew how to ask politely.

Ah, pizza . . .
So beautiful, you could hang it on the wall of a museum.

So convenient, you could
eat it in the bathtub.

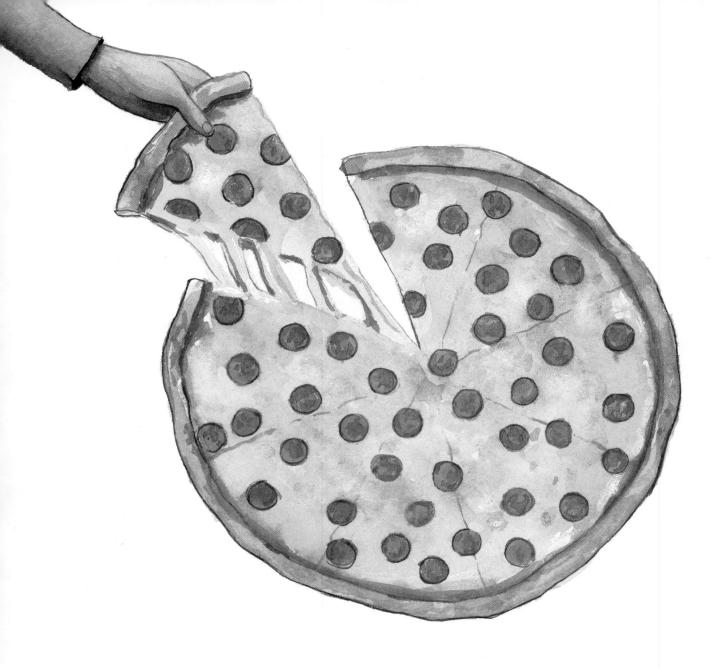

Of course, the best part about pizza is the gooey cheesy-ness, salty pepperoni-ness, sweet, sweet tomato-ness, and crispity, crunchity crust.

Yum!

Sorry, Raccoon. I didn't mean to rub it in.

Hey, cheer up. I just had a great idea! Let's throw a pizza party at your house tonight.

Shhh, don't tell anyone. This will be a secret pizza party.

I know what you're thinking. Why would we keep such a delicious, delicious party a secret?

Okay, sure. It's so folks don't show up to bonk you with brooms, but that's not the only reason. When you make something secret, you make it special.

Regular handshake: Boring.

Secret handshake: *Booyah!*

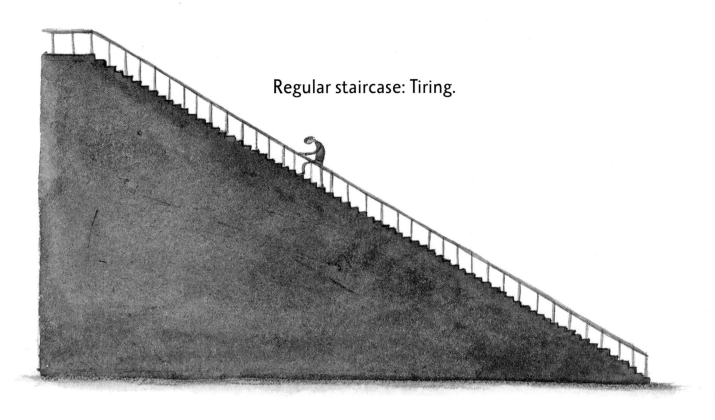

Regular staircase: Tiring.

Secret staircase: Terrific!

Regular pizza party: Get that raccoon off the table!!!

Secret pizza party: Get that raccoon another slice of pizza, he's the guest of honor.

Hot diggity dog, our pizza party is going to be so much fun!
Call the pizza man and tell him to bring over his absolute finest pizza pie.

Hang on a minute, you don't want the
delivery guy to know where you live.
He might recognize you from the
posters and chase you off
with a broom.

Think, Raccoon. **Think!**

SILVERMAN'S
BEARD STORE
LUMBERJACK $31.50
SANTA $9.99
Uncle Mark's PIZZA
PIZ
ITALIAN ICES
OPEN
USED MITTEN

Okay now, play it cool. You're just an honest pizza-buying citizen who left his wallet in the car. The pizza man thinks you'll be right back . . .

Let's go!

I've planned the perfect getaway route:

Around the broom factory.

WE MAKE BROOMS

Over the broom enthusiasts club.

MEETING TONIGHT: THE BROOM ENTHUSIASTS CLUB

Run, Raccoon.

Run like the wind!

Phew! We made it.
Let's barricade the doors and pop open that pizza box.
Mmmmm . . .

SECRET PIZZA PARTY!
Oops, I said that kind of loud.
Sorry, pizza smell gives me the happy screams.

Try not to crunch too loud.
Definitely no high-fiving.
Or music.
Or dancing.
In fact, we'd better turn off the lights and whisper,
just to be safe . . .

secret pizza party!

What's the matter?

Sweet sassy molassy, look at all that pizza!

Clearly, these people are much better at throwing parties than they are at keeping secrets.

Are you thinking what I'm thinking?

SECRET